Welcome to The Giggle Club

D0537989

The Giggle Club is a collection of new picture books made to put a giggle into early reading. There are funny stories about a contrary mouse, a dancing fox, a turtle with a trumpet, a pig with a ball, a hungry monster, a laughing lobster, an elephant who sneezes away the jungle and lots more! Each of these characters is a member of **The Giggle Club**, but anyone can join: just pick up a **Giggle Club** book, read it and get giggling!

Turn to the checklist on the inside back cover and tick off the Giggle Club books you have read.

TEE HEE!

HA HA!

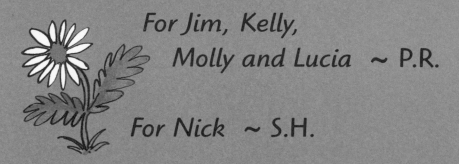

For Jim, Kelly,
Molly and Lucia ~ P.R.

For Nick ~ S.H.

First published 1996 by Walker Books Ltd
87 Vauxhall Walk, London SE11 5HJ

This edition published 1997

10 9 8 7 6 5 4 3

Text © 1996 Phyllis Root
Illustrations © 1996 Sue Heap

Printed in Hong Kong

This book has been typeset in Highlander Book.

British Library Cataloguing in Publication Data
A catalogue record for this book
is available from the British Library.

ISBN 0-7445-5462-4

THE HUNGRY MONSTER

Written by
Phyllis Root

Illustrated by
Sue Heap

WALKER BOOKS
AND SUBSIDIARIES
LONDON • BOSTON • SYDNEY

A rocket came to Planet Earth.
Out stepped a monster.

"HUNGRY!" roared the monster.

The monster
saw a daisy.
"YUM!" said the monster.

The monster tasted
the daisy.

"YUCK!" said the monster.

**"REALLY
HUNGRY!"**
roared the monster.
The monster saw a rock.
"YUM!" said the monster.

The monster tasted
the rock.

"YUCK!" said the monster.

"REALLY, REALLY HUNGRY!"
roared the monster.
The monster saw a tree.
"YUM!" said the monster.

The monster tasted the tree.

"YUCK!" said the monster.

"REALLY, REALLY, REALLY HUNGRY!" roared the monster.

The monster
saw a girl...

"**YUM!**" said the monster.

The monster ate the banana,
skin and all.

"YUCK!" said the girl.